ANGEL HOUSE

Written by Anne Curtis
Illustrated by Chris Corner

Collins

They say I'm not like them.
They say I'm different.

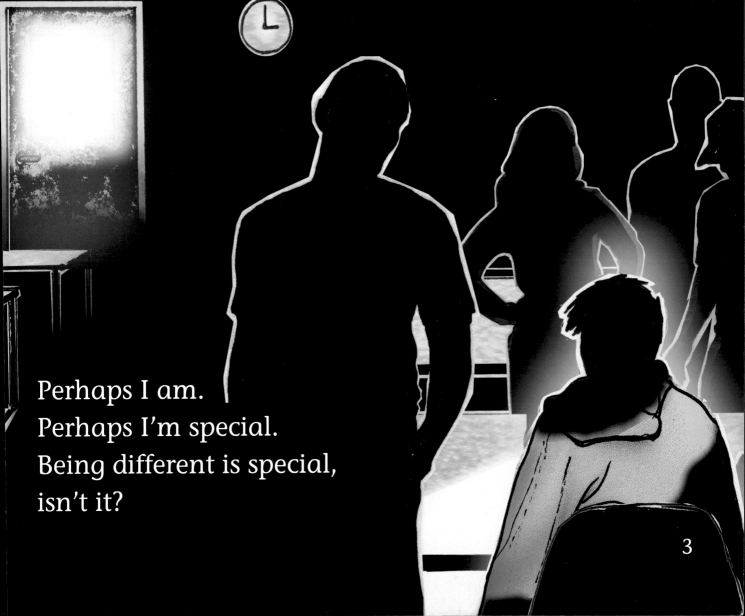

Perhaps I am.
Perhaps I'm special.
Being different is special,
isn't it?

3

There are times I feel I don't belong.
There are times I need to be on my own.

4

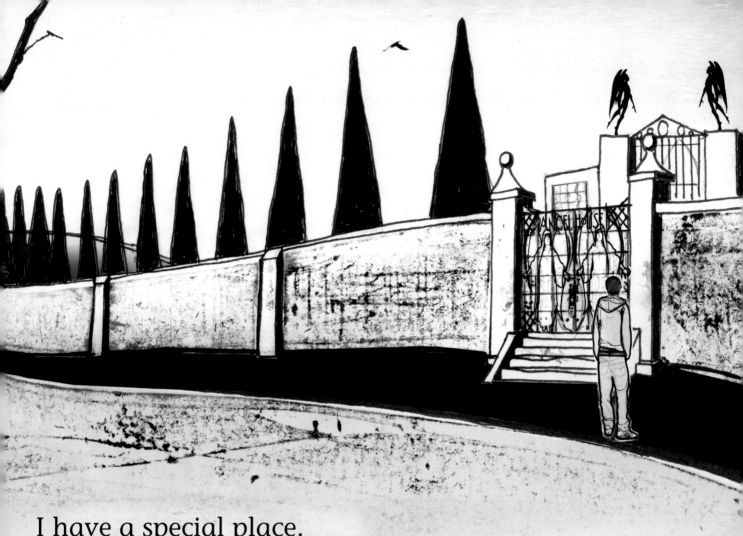

I have a special place.

There's an old house near where I live.
The house has big metal gates.

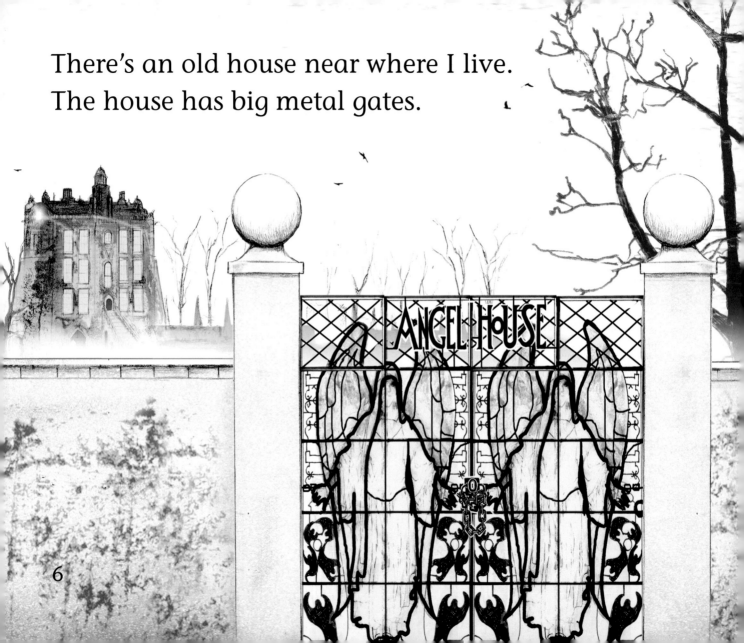

On the gates are the words *Angel House*.

No one lives at Angel House. It's empty.
Angel House is like a huge, dark flower
in a wild garden.

The path is covered with grass.
The grass reaches past my waist.

There are angels carved
above the door.
More angels are painted
on the glass windows.

When I step inside,
the house is still and quiet.
When I step inside,
I feel different.

Hundreds of small, white feathers.

I hold out my hands as if I'm catching snowflakes.
The feathers feel soft and warm.

They feel like the wings of
a small, white bird.

Bright light shines from the roof.
It lights up the stairs.

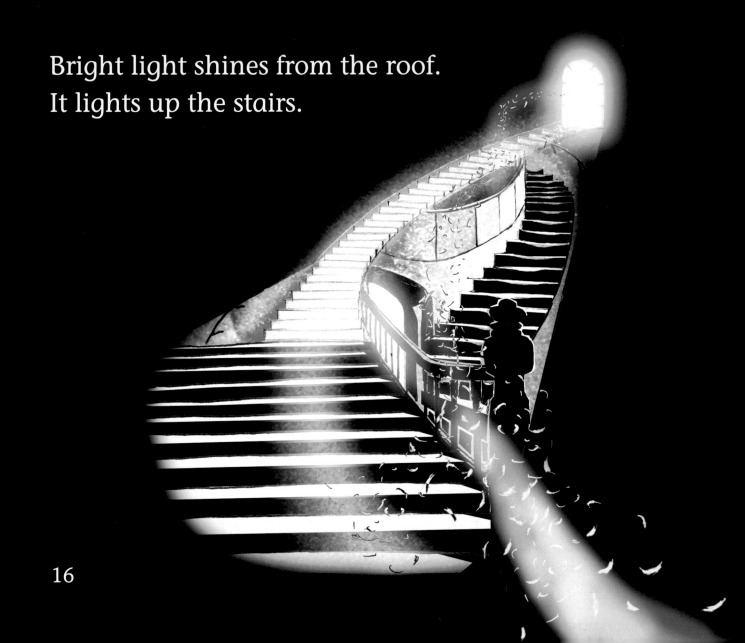

Up and up I climb, through a storm of feathers.

On the roof, I can see for miles.

I'm like a bird sitting in a nest.

In Angel House, I know I'm not like other boys.
If I spread my arms, you can see my feathers.

Look! I have wings.
Watch me fly!

Feelings staircase

weakness

loneliness

peacefulness

security

I'm not
like them.

I feel I don't
belong.

I have
a special
place …
still and
quiet.

The feathers
feel soft
and warm.

22

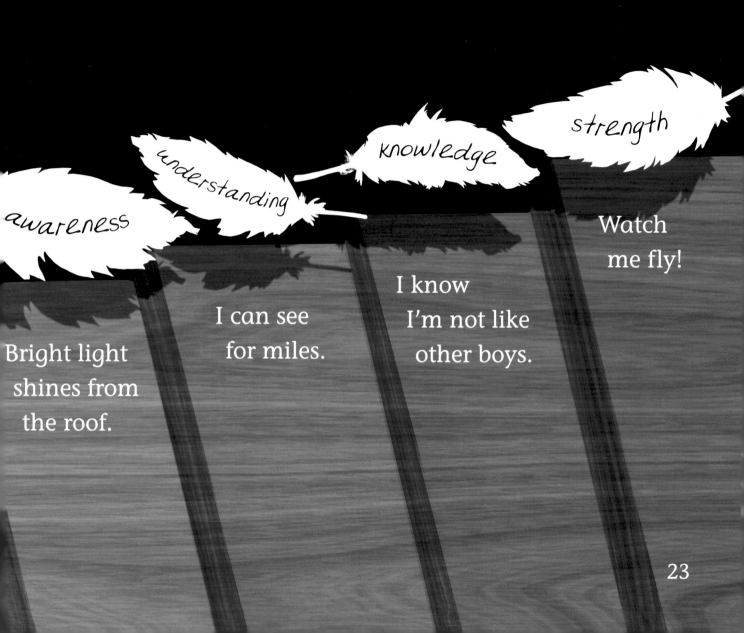

awareness

understanding

knowledge

strength

Bright light shines from the roof.

I can see for miles.

I know I'm not like other boys.

Watch me fly!

23

Ideas for reading

Written by Gillian Howell
Primary Literacy Consultant

Learning objectives: *(reading objectives correspond with Green band; all other objectives correspond with Diamond band)* use phonics to read unknown or difficult words; appraise a text quickly, deciding on its value/quality/usefulness; understand underlying themes, causes and points of view; use the techniques of dialogic talk to explore ideas, topics or issues; integrate words, images and sounds imaginatively for different purposes

Curriculum links: Citizenship: Taking part; Citizenship: Choices

High frequency words: house, there, times, don't, be, have, an, old, where, live, has, one, with, more, when, from, as, white, out, if, not

Interest words: angel, different, special, empty, flower, quiet, feathers, snowflakes, light, climb

Resources: paper, pens, pencils

Word count: 290

Getting started

- Look at the cover and ask the children to give a personal response to the illustration. What impression does the picture of the house give them about the book? Have they ever seen a house like this? What do they think might be inside?

- Ask them to predict what sort of story they think this will be and give a reason for their opinions, e.g. *a spooky story because the house looks scary.*

- Read the back cover blurb. Discuss the first person "I" usage. Ask them who they think the narrator of the story will be and who "they" might be.

Reading and responding

- Ask the children to read the story in pairs. Remind them to use their knowledge of phonics to work out new words. If necessary, prompt the children to use *sh* in *special.*

- On pp2–3, ask the children to say where the story begins. Ask how the narrator feels about this place and what gives them that impression. Ask them to focus on the shadowy figures in the picture. Can they think of any adjectives to describe them, e.g. threatening, aggressive, bullying?

- Remind the children to look closely at the illustrations. Discuss how they are an important part of the story, e.g. *What do they tell us about the atmosphere in the room on pp2–3?*

- Ask the children to read to the end of the story. Praise and support them as they read.